CUTTING-EDGE CAREERS™

CAREERS IN
BIOTECHNOLOGY

Linley Erin Hall

ROSEN
PUBLISHING®

New York

Published in 2007 by The Rosen Publishing Group, Inc.
29 East 21st Street, New York, NY 10010

First Edition

Library of Congress Cataloging-in-Publication Data

Hall, Linley Erin.
Careers in biotechnology / Linley Erin Hall. — 1st ed.
　　p. cm. — (Cutting-edge careers)
Includes bibliographical references and index.
ISBN-13: 978-1-4042-0954-1
ISBN-10: 1-4042-0954-9 (library binding)
1. Biotechnology — Vocational guidance — Juvenile literature. I. Title.

TP248.218.H35 2007
660.6023 — dc22

　　　　　　　　　　　　　　　　　　　　　　　　　2006018933

Manufactured in the United States of America

CONTENTS

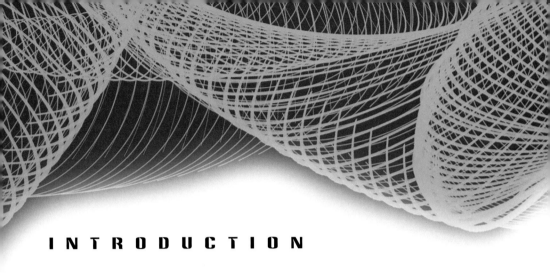

INTRODUCTION

[T]he word "biotechnology" seems to be cropping up everywhere these days. But what is it? Very simply, biotechnology is the application of technology to the living world. It is the manipulation of living things to create products, processes, and services.

Some people have said that the twenty-first century is the century of biotechnology. But humans have been using biotechnology for a long time. For example, both yeast and mold are types of fungi, a kind of living creature. Yeast makes bread rise. Molds are important in making cheese. Bread and cheese are human-made products that require the manipulation of living things. They are examples of biotechnology that date back 6,000 years.

Karl Ereky, a Hungarian engineer, coined the word "biotechnology" in 1919. He intended it to mean all the ways that products are made with the help of living things. Today, many biotechnology products are made in ways that Ereky could not have imagined in 1919. Scientists have learned a lot in the more than eight decades since then.

Living things are also called organisms. Organisms are made of cells, tiny compartments that contain water and chemicals essential to life. Some organisms, like bacteria, have only one cell. The human body contains trillions of cells, and every one of these cells contains DNA.

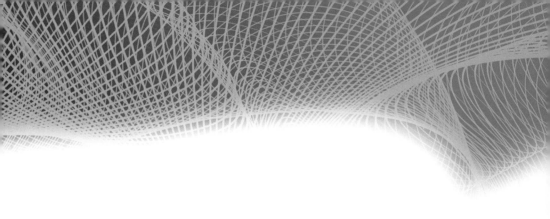

DNA is short for deoxyribonucleic acid. It contains the instructions for making proteins. Proteins perform the work that takes place in cells. Different sections of DNA contain the instructions for different proteins. These sections are called genes. Genetics is the study of genes.

DNA is passed down from parents to their children. A child gets some of her DNA from her mother and some from her father. The DNA of two humans is much more similar to each other than the DNA of a human and a cow, or a cow and a tomato. But the relatively small differences in human DNA cause people to have often strikingly different characteristics. DNA determines hair and eye color, for example, as well as height and complexion.

Much of biotechnology involves manipulating DNA. This is often called genetic engineering. Researchers can take a useful gene from one organism and put it into a completely different organism. The new gene gives the organism new characteristics. It might make a plant larger or more nutritious. Scientists can also remove genes from an organism or change genes in an organism. Genetically modified organisms, or GMOs, have had their DNA altered in some way by biotechnology.

A good example of a GMO is golden rice, which is genetically engineered to boost its nutritional value. Golden rice contains three genes from other organisms—two from the daffodil and one from maize (corn). These genes give the rice plant the ability to make beta-carotene in the part of the plant that people eat. The human body turns beta-carotene into vitamin A. People in many developing

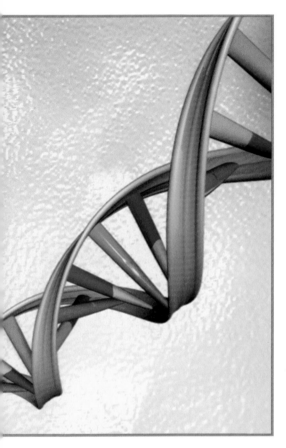

DNA, short for deoxyribonucleic acid, contains the instructions for making proteins in cells. Much of the research in biotechnology involves manipulating DNA.

countries do not get enough vitamin A. This deficiency can lead to blindness and other serious illnesses, even death. Researchers hope that golden rice can reduce the number of people with vitamin A deficiencies in areas where rice is a staple food.

Some GMOs, like golden rice, are intended for human consumption. Other GMOs are used to make different kinds of products. For example, researchers can modify bacteria to produce proteins and other chemicals that are useful to humans. These materials include drugs, vaccines, and food additives. Biotechnology may also be able to improve human health by providing patients with healthy genes to replace genes that are unhealthy and malfunctioning, resulting in disease.

Biotechnology is most often used to improve agriculture and human health, but biotechnology is also being used in other areas.

A plant biotechnologist examines a golden rice plant. Golden rice is a genetically modified organism that contains extra genes to make it more nutritious.

Environmental biotechnology puts bacteria to work cleaning up pollution. Researchers are also trying to use bacteria to produce energy. Chapter 1 will look at some of these different areas of research.

With so much going on in biotechnology, the range of careers available is extremely wide. People are needed in the laboratory to create GMOs and gene therapies. But people also work in biotechnology factories, run tests of new drugs and other medical treatments, write about biotechnology, sell products, and make sure that biotechnology is safe. Chapter 2 explores some of these careers, and chapter 3 discusses the education needed to achieve them.

Biotechnology is a growing industry. It is also a controversial one. Some people believe that products made with biotechnology could be harmful to the environment or to human health. Other people worry that biotechnology may be used in ways that are unethical. Chapter 4 will take a closer look at some of these controversies. It will also explore what the future of biotechnology might look like and what new careers may be opening up.

CHAPTER 1

Areas of Biotechnology Research

Biotechnology has been applied to many industries. Agriculture and health care are the best known. But biotechnology is being used more and more to produce useful materials, clean up the environment, and solve crimes. Within each of these fields, biotechnology can be used in many ways. This chapter will look at the basic techniques that scientists working in biotechnology often use. It will also explore the applications of biotechnology in different fields.

Basic Techniques of Biotechnology

Most research in biotechnology is based on changing or moving the DNA of organisms. Recombinant DNA technologies are those that allow researchers to break and rejoin DNA, as well as to make lots of it. This process lets scientists isolate one gene in an organism so that they can study it. The next step is usually to alter the gene and/or put it in another organism.

Recombinant DNA technologies are the basis for much of the work in biotechnology labs. The steps often include:

Growing cells in a glass dish, outside an organism

Isolating a gene from those cells

Inserting that gene into the cells of a different organism

Testing if the new gene is working in the cells of the second organism

The next step is to test the new gene in an actual organism. Microorganisms such as bacteria have just one cell. Once a new gene is inserted into that one cell, it's in the organism and should be functioning. But other, more complex organisms have billions or trillions of cells. Often, the new gene needs to be in each one of those cells. For most plants and animals, the easiest way to do this is to insert the gene into an egg or embryo. As an embryo grows and develops into a mature organism, its cells divide. During cell division, a second copy of the cell's DNA is made so that the two new cells each have a copy. The new gene inserted by researchers into the original cell is copied at the same time. In this way, all cells in the organism will end up with the new gene.

Industrial Biotechnology

Industrial biotechnology is also known as microbial biotechnology and industrial microbiology. This area of biotechnology puts microorganisms

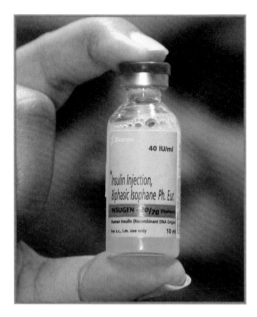

Biotechnology has allowed insulin, a treatment for diabetics, to be produced more cheaply and efficiently. This insulin is made by yeast that contains the gene for human insulin.

such as bacteria and fungi to work making products for humans. Researchers use recombinant DNA technologies to put new genes in the microorganisms. Scientists can also insert stretches of DNA that tell the cells to produce lots of the protein made from the new gene. This turns a bacterium into a tiny factory for making a particular protein or a material that is derived from certain proteins. The protein or other chemical can then be collected from the microorganism and sold.

Insulin was the first protein to be made this way. Insulin helps adjust the amount of sugar in the blood. Cells in the human pancreas normally produce insulin, but people who have diabetes do not make enough of it. For many years, diabetics were injected with insulin taken from the pancreases of pigs or cows. In the 1970s, researchers used recombinant DNA technology to insert the gene for human insulin into a bacterium. The bacterium then produces insulin, which diabetics can inject into their bloodstream.

Bacteria and fungi now produce many proteins for human use. Many of these are products that are important in health care, like antibiotics and vaccines. Drugs used to be made with chemicals, and some still are. But using microorganisms to make drugs is often less expensive and produces less waste.

Microorganisms have even been used to produce medicines and other treatments for pets and livestock. For example, bovine growth hormone is a chemical that naturally occurs in cows and is important to their milk production. Researchers have used bacteria to make supplemental bovine growth hormone. When injected into cows, it increases the amount of milk they produce. This allows dairy farmers to create more product and derive more profit from each cow.

Microorganisms also produce many other materials. These include flavorings and other food additives, chemicals, and enzymes. Enzymes are proteins that speed up chemical reactions. These enzymes are used in many products, including laundry detergent and dishwashing soap.

Health Care

In addition to the use of recombinant DNA to make bacteria produce medicines, biotechnology can improve human health in other ways. A mutation is a change in an organism's DNA. Sometimes, mutations lead to characteristics that are good for the organism. Other times, mutations can cause disease. Gene therapy is a kind of biotechnology that introduces healthy genes into humans to counteract malfunctioning, disease-causing genes.

Designing a gene therapy is a multistep process. First, an appropriate gene for the treatment must be identified. Researchers must then create and purify large quantities of it. Next, they must figure out how to get it into living cells. The treatment must be tested on cells grown outside organisms, then on animals, and finally on humans.

Gene therapy does not replace the unhealthy gene. It supplements it with a healthy gene that can make useful proteins. Researchers hope that the healthy gene will be able to reduce the effect of the unhealthy gene.

Tests of some gene therapies have caused illness or death among some humans who have volunteered for medical trials. China is the only country that has approved a gene therapy, targeted at head and neck cancers, for widespread use. But many companies are currently designing and testing gene therapies for humans. Gene therapy has also been used to successfully treat genetic blindness and blood clotting disorders in dogs.

Genetically Engineered Plants

Biotechnology is becoming more important in agriculture. Genetic engineering can add many desirable characteristics to plants. For example, it can make foods more nutritious. As mentioned in the introduction, golden rice has been genetically engineered to have high levels of beta-carotene. The human body turns this beta-carotene into vitamin A.

Biotechnology can also alter the amount of herbicides and pesticides needed to successfully raise a crop. Herbicides are used on crops to kill weeds, and pesticides are sprayed on crops to kill insects. Yet these chemicals can be toxic and get into the soil and water system. They are also widely believed to cause various kinds of cancers and other illnesses in humans.

Herbicides can even be toxic enough to kill the plants they are meant to protect. Cotton is a crop that has been vulnerable to herbicides and has benefited from the bioengineering of herbicides. Roundup Ready, a variety of bioengineered cotton, contains a gene from a bacterium commonly found in the soil. It makes the plant resistant to the herbicide Roundup. Roundup kills ordinary cotton plants. But Roundup can be used on Roundup Ready cotton to kill weeds without affecting the cotton plant.

A worker harvests Roundup Ready cotton on a farm in Mississippi. The cotton has been genetically modified to be more resistant to the herbicide Roundup.

Another type of bioengineered cotton, Bt cotton, contains a gene from a different bacterium. This gene causes the plant to make a pesticide that kills bollworms and budworms. These are the most common cotton-eating pests in many areas. Since the pesticide is produced by the gene from the bacterium and is already contained in the plant, farmers don't need to spray it on their crops. The soil, water supply, and farm workers are kept safe from contact with the Bt toxin.

In the future, many other special characteristics could be introduced into plants through genetic engineering. Genetic engineering could produce plants that are larger, more resistant to cold, or require less water. If bigger, more numerous plants that grew in relatively dry areas could be produced, it could have great benefits to typically drought- and famine-stricken areas. Some scientists are also combining agricultural and human health research. They are genetically engineering plants to make vaccines and other drugs. In the future, an apple a day really could keep the doctor away.

Genetically Engineered Animals

For thousands of years, people have tried to introduce desirable characteristics into animals by selectively mating male and female animals with those valued traits. Biotechnology can introduce many of those characteristics into animals much faster and more efficiently than breeding can (breeding for desirable characteristics to begin manifesting themselves takes many generations). Animals may be genetically engineered to grow faster, not get sick as often, or have meat that is more nutritious or tasty.

Like plants, animals can also be genetically engineered to produce medicine in their milk, blood, or other tissues. But many animals also have organs that are similar to those of humans. Organ transplants between different mammals, like humans and pigs, have been tried. But the human body recognizes the organ as foreign and attacks it in a process called rejection. Researchers are trying to create pigs that lack the chemicals that cause the human body to reject pig organs. This could make organ transplants between humans and animals possible, which would increase the number of organs available for transplanting.

Cloning

Reproductive cloning creates an individual with the exact same DNA as another individual. Cloned animals have been created by first

These pigs were cloned from adult pigs by a British company that has also cloned sheep.

removing the DNA from an egg cell. Then the DNA from a regular cell, one not involved in reproduction, is put in the egg. Researchers make the cell divide using chemicals or an electric current. Eventually, the embryo is put in a female animal, where it develops until it is born. The DNA donor and the clone are genetically identical; they have the exact same DNA. But a clone may not look or act quite the same as the donor because of differing environmental influences. Animals that have been cloned in recent years include sheep, cats, cows, mice, and pigs.

Reproductive cloning could be used to increase the numbers of endangered animals. It could also be used to bring extinct animals back to life if researchers are able to discover intact DNA from among their preserved remains.

Many people think that cloning is new. But humans have been cloning plants for thousands of years. If one cuts off part of a plant and puts it in water or fresh soil, it will often grow roots and begin to function on its own. The new plant is genetically identical to the original one. In addition, cloning of animals has been happening since the 1950s. The difference is that researchers now use adult cells instead of cells from embryos.

Therapeutic cloning is used to create embryos from which researchers can remove stem cells. Stem cells are cells that can become any kind of specialized cell, like heart, lung, or kidney cells. Stem cells could be used to grow new organs or replace diseased tissue. But stem cells are very controversial. Chapter 4 will talk more about them and the debate surrounding their use.

Environmental Biotechnology

Environmental groups sometimes portray biotechnology as a threat to the environment. But biotechnology can also benefit the environment. Bacteria and fungi are being used to clean up toxic waste, and bacteria may also be a useful source of energy in the future.

Some bacteria can get energy and nutrition from chemicals that are dangerous to humans. They take in these dangerous chemicals—removing them from the soil, water, or atmosphere—and release harmless ones as waste. Many researchers are using these bacteria to clean up polluted water and land. Sometimes, the bacteria are genetically engineered so that they can do the cleanup faster or more efficiently.

Bacteria may also be able to help solve the world's energy needs. Some bacteria naturally carry out reactions that produce energy. These bacteria could be used to provide electricity. Some bacteria even produce electricity while also breaking down dangerous chemicals. In the future, bacteria could clean some pollutants out of water and provide electricity for other cleanup jobs at the same time.

Cutting Edge Careers
Careers
Cutting Edge Careers

Jobs in Biotechnology

At the end of 2003, there were nearly 1,500 biotechnology companies in the United States, according to the Biotechnology Industry Organization. These companies employed nearly 200,000 people in various positions.

Most biotechnology companies are small. Many have fewer than 100 employees. Larger companies may also work in areas other than biotechnology. For example, a pharmaceutical company might make some drugs using biotechnology but others through more traditional chemical processes. New biotechnology companies open regularly. Many have not sold anything yet because they are still developing their product. It can take ten to fifteen years for a biotechnology offering to move from an idea initially experimented with and

Researchers analyze samples of genetically engineered hybrid corn *(above)*. Inserting genes from one plant into another plant can make crops larger, more nutritious, or more resistant to drought.

developed in the lab to a fully tested and government-approved product in the customer's hands.

According to a report prepared by Business Insights in 2005, the top ten biotechnology companies are Amgen, Genentech, Serono, Biogen Idec, UCB-Celltech, Genzyme, Gilead, MedImmune, Chiron, and Millenium. Many different positions are available at these and other biotechnology companies. The rest of this chapter looks at some of the major jobs within the field of biotechnology.

Research and Development

The laboratory is the heart of every biotechnology company. Research and development—also known as R&D—is how researchers discover new knowledge and turn it into useful products, processes, and services. According to the Biotechnology Industry Organization, the biotechnology industry spent $17.9 billion on research and development in 2003. This makes biotechnology one of the world's most research-intensive industries.

A lot of biotechnology research takes place at colleges and universities. Companies may make the products, but the ideas behind them often come from universities. According to Bio Economic Research Associates, twelve of the top thirty-five organizations that conduct biotechnology research are universities.

R&D positions can be roughly divided into three categories based on education and experience. Senior research scientists direct the research. They decide which projects their laboratory will work on, and they supervise other researchers. Research scientists also conduct research, interpret the results, write reports on experiments, and attend scientific conferences. They almost always hold doctoral degrees (advanced degrees awarded after four or more years of specialized study following college).

Research associates, sometimes called research assistants, collaborate with others to perform research. They conduct experiments, make observations, analyze data, and reach conclusions. Research associates also write reports about their work. They may discover new ideas that lead to the development of new products. They usually hold bachelor's degrees (awarded after four years of college study) or master's degrees (awarded after a year or two of specialized study following college).

Technicians, also called laboratory assistants, write detailed observations about experiments. They may analyze results and draw conclusions from them. They may also write reports about their work. Some technicians order and maintain lab supplies or equipment. Others may care for animals or plants in the lab. They usually have associate's degrees (usually received after two years of study at a community or technical college) or bachelor's degrees.

In general, the more education and experience you have, the greater your chances of landing a position that offers you more independence and responsibility. People with doctoral degrees have worked in labs for many years. They know what sorts of questions to ask and strategies to employ. Therefore, they generally become lab and project supervisors. Technicians with associate's degrees do not have nearly as extensive backgrounds. Therefore, they are limited by their supervisors in the tasks they are allowed to perform, the decisions they can make, and the freedom they have to experiment in the lab. They generally follow the orders of the supervisor and complete tasks assigned to them. They have little say in how to design or conduct lab projects. It's not uncommon for someone to work as a technician or research assistant for a few years, then decide to go back to school to gain the experience and skills needed for a more important position in the laboratory.

A variety of skills are important for success in the laboratory. Attention to detail is necessary. An entire experiment can be ruined

A college student works in a genetics laboratory at the University of Arizona. Research careers often involve long hours and performing the same experiment many times.

and data made meaningless or misleading if one small step is skipped or botched. Researchers need to be careful observers as well. A lot of lab work involves recording what is seen during experiments. In addition, researchers often perform the same procedures over and over again. They may work with different genes, but use the same techniques on each of them. Students interested in research careers should have a long attention span and not get bored easily.

Researchers in environmental biotechnology and some other biotech areas may perform fieldwork. This means that they conduct experiments outside the laboratory. This could be on a farm or at a polluted river. Students who enjoy travel and the outdoors are most suited for fieldwork.

Researchers must also be able to accept failure. Experiments rarely work perfectly on the first try. Sometimes, they don't work at all. Scientists often must develop new approaches in the wake of failed experiments, or even start from scratch. Flexibility is important. So is commitment. Many people in biotechnology R&D work far more than forty hours per week, which is the standard workweek.

Clinical Trials

A clinical trial is a test of a drug, vaccine, or other medical treatment on human beings. Clinical trials do not begin until tests on animals have suggested the treatment is safe. But since animals may react differently to a drug than humans will, testing on people is essential if the drug is ever to be manufactured and sold for human use.

Clinical trials of a drug's effects and effectiveness on humans occur in several phases. A Phase I trial tests a drug on twenty to eighty people to determine its safety, pinpoint the ideal dosage, and identify any negative side effects. A Phase II trial tests a drug on 100 to 300 people to see if it does what it was designed to do. This second testing phase also provides additional opportunities to determine the drug's safety. A Phase III trial tests a drug on 1,000 to 3,000 people to confirm that it is effective, and to compare its effectiveness and side effects to other treatments of the same condition, disease, or disorder. If the results of the trials are positive, then the U.S. Food and Drug Administration (FDA) will approve the drug. The company can then sell it to the public.

People who work in clinical trials design the testing program, including patient surveys, consent forms, and other documents. They work with the doctors and nurses who monitor and care for the patients to make sure the correct procedures are followed. Workers also collect data from the trial and analyze it to see if the medical treatment works or not. Jobs related to clinical trials include clinical research associate, clinical coordinator, clinical data manager, and clinical programmer. These positions generally require bachelor's degrees.

Clinical programmers design and build computer databases to hold all the information gathered during a clinical trial. The health of patients may be followed for months or years. At each study session, patients may undergo several medical tests and fill out surveys about their health. Clinical programmers make sure that information from each phase of the trial gets entered in the study databases. They also analyze the data and resolve problems with it or the database.

Clinical trials are important in making sure that a drug is safe and effective before many patients begin to use it. As long as companies continue to create new drugs, clinical trial workers will continue to be needed.

Computer-Related Jobs

Employees with computer skills are needed in areas other than clinical trials. Bioinformatics is the use of computers to gain new information about DNA and proteins. Computers can compare DNA from different organisms. Based on a protein's shape, computers can predict how it will function in a cell. Computers can also analyze the observations and results from experiments. Humans can do many of these things, too, but computers are often faster, more accurate, and more efficient. Humans must still create the software that allows computers to do these things, however, and software designing is a thriving field.

Biotechnology companies hire people who know about both computers and biology to perform many different jobs. Some employees write software designed to gain information about DNA and proteins or to analyze data. Others create and update databases of biological information. Still others perform essential maintenance and repairs on the computers used in laboratories and elsewhere in the company. Education and interest in both biotechnology and computer science are important for these positions.

Patents

When a company develops a new product, it will often want to apply for a patent. A patent is a government document that gives the holder the exclusive right to make and sell a product, usually for a period of twenty years. After twenty years have passed, any manufacturer can create copies of your invention or product and sell it in direct competition with you. Lawyers and patent agents prepare the documents necessary to acquire patents. Lawyers also assist biotechnology companies in forging collaborations with other companies and drafting confidentiality agreements and other legal documents. Patent agents need bachelor's degrees, and lawyers require law degrees.

Quality Control

An essential part of any biotechnology business is quality control. Quality control analysts test materials and review the results to make sure that the materials meet company, industry, and government standards. Any that do not must be discarded. Quality control engineers develop the procedures used to test and evaluate materials. They may also set the standards that the materials must achieve. These engineers often train other workers on how to use these procedures.

Many careers are available in biotechnology other than research and development. Here a worker collects pills in a drug manufacturing plant in preparation for packaging.

A lot of quality control in biotechnology is laboratory work. As a result, it requires similar skills as those used in research and development. A bachelor's degree is also required.

Manufacturing

After a product has been fully tested and approved, it must be produced in a factory. This may require changes in how the product is made. For example, in the laboratory, researchers might keep bacteria that were producing an antibiotic in a small container. However, it doesn't make sense to have lots of small containers in a factory. Large vats are more appropriate. But the bacteria may act differently when in a large vat instead of a small container. Development engineers would have to find a way to store the bacteria in large vats without affecting the bacteria's performance or behavior. Development engineers devise new methods and technologies tailored to the conditions of factory storage and manufacture. These engineers also help design and start up new factories to make sure that things run smoothly from the start.

Many other jobs are available in biotechnology manufacturing. Engineers make sure that a wide variety of processes are as efficient as possible. Schedulers make sure that raw materials are ordered and products are produced on schedule. Other workers may create and put on product labels, operate production equipment, or test the quality of products.

Manufacturing technicians may not need more than a high school diploma. Other positions generally require at least a bachelor's degree, often in engineering. Engineering jobs are good for students who like to solve problems and work with their hands.

Sales and Marketing

Once a company has developed and manufactured a product, sales representatives try to sell it to businesses, doctors, or directly to the public. People in marketing create print, radio, and television advertisements, brochures, Web sites, and other sources of information about products. Biotechnology sales representatives usually have a degree in an area of biology. A degree in communications, marketing, or business can also be helpful.

Teaching

Finally, colleges, universities, and high schools need people to teach classes on biotechnology. This helps ensure that some students will

A sales representative tries to interest a doctor in his company's product. People who sell biotechnology products need a strong background in science as well as sales.

learn about the various fields, become interested, pursue biotechnology studies, and eventually enter the workforce and fill positions in the industry.

Obviously, lots of different positions are available in biotechnology. The next chapter will look at the education needed to get these jobs.

CHAPTER 3

Cutting Edge Careers
Cutting Edge Careers
Careers
Cutting Edge Careers

The Education Path for a Biotech Career

Getting the right education is important for success in any field. It is possible to pursue a career in biotechnology with only a high school diploma. Most positions require some sort of college degree, however, ranging from a two-year associate's degree from a community college to a doctoral degree.

Many opportunities to learn about biotechnology exist both inside and outside the classroom. This chapter will examine many of them.

Before College

Preparation for a career in biotechnology can begin at an early age. You should definitely begin laying the groundwork by high

A strong foundation in mathematics is important for success in biotechnology. High school students should also take biology, chemistry, physics, and English classes.

school, however. Many universities recommend that college-bound students take four years of English, three years of science, and four years of mathematics in high school. Students interested in biotechnology should take four years of science if possible, including biology, chemistry, and physics. Mathematics classes should include algebra, geometry, trigonometry, and introductory calculus. Small high schools may not offer classes such as calculus or physics. Students may be able to take these courses at a local community college instead.

Four years of English are important because people in biotechnology spend a lot of time communicating ideas and results to others. The success of an idea or proposal depends on your ability to express it clearly, accurately, and articulately. Writing for the school newspaper, yearbook, or literary magazine can help improve writing skills. Scientists frequently make presentations and write journal articles based on their research studies. Students can prepare for this kind of professional activity by taking courses in public speaking or participating on a debate team. This will make them more comfortable in front of an audience and help them write clearly and persuasively.

As college admissions become more and more competitive, good grades are ever more important. So is the level of difficulty of the coursework. Students should take honors, advanced placement, or international baccalaureate courses if offered by their school. This is often true even if a student is likely to get a B in an advanced course instead of an A in a regular-level class.

Some schools offer classes in biotechnology as part of the regular curriculum. Others have biotechnology clubs or after-school workshops. These classes and other programs often provide hands-on lab experience. This can be very useful in helping to figuring out if research and development is the right career path for you.

Another way to learn more about biotechnology is through a local university. Many universities have outreach programs for middle and high school students. These may include tours, classroom lab activities, workshops on the college campus, or summer classes. Universities also hold lectures that are open to the public. In these lectures, researchers often talk about the work taking place in their laboratories.

Students should also read articles and watch documentaries and news reports about biotechnology. Scientists report new discoveries every day. The media also provides information about companies, new products, and controversies. Books almost always offer the most in-depth and comprehensive information available. But because of

Students should try to obtain as much hands-on laboratory experience as possible. High schools, community colleges, local universities, and other groups may offer programs related to biotechnology.

the length of the publishing process, they do not always contain the most current information, even when they are brand new. In a cutting-edge field such as biotechnology, a lot can change in the six months to a year that it takes for a manuscript to be edited, printed, and published. So reading newspaper, magazine, and journal articles is essential for keeping current.

To hone their research, creative, problem-solving, and engineering skills, students may also want to get involved in science fairs and other academic competitions. These often require students to carry out a research project, and then present findings or a finished product.

This is excellent practice for the actual research and development you may someday be conducting in a biotechnology job.

Undergraduate Degrees

Many community, technical, and junior colleges offer two-year associate's degrees in biotechnology and related fields. These associate of applied science degrees focus on practical laboratory skills that are in high demand within the industry. This means that graduates often find jobs as technicians soon after graduation. Without a bachelor's degree or more, however, opportunities for advancement are limited.

Most universities do not offer four-year undergraduate degrees in biotechnology. Instead, most students interested in biotechnology complete an undergraduate degree in a broader field of life or chemical sciences, or in engineering. The particular major a student chooses depends on what aspect of biotechnology interests him or her most. Potential college majors include:

Animal Science

Biochemistry

Bioengineering

Bioinformatics

Biology

Botany or Plant Biology

Cell Biology

———— Chemical Engineering

———— Computational Biology

———— Environmental Science

———— Food Science

———— Forestry

———— Genetics

———— Microbiology

———— Molecular Biology

———— Zoology

Some universities do offer majors in biotechnology, but each focuses on a very specific area of the field. The University of California–Los Angeles (UCLA) offers a plant biotechnology major through its College of Letters and Science. The University of California–San Diego offers a major in bioengineering: biotechnology through its Jacobs School of Engineering. The University of Nevada offers a major in animal biotechnology through its School of Veterinary Medicine. Each of these majors will teach different, specialized skills and prepare students for a different, distinct area of biotechnology.

Some universities, like North Carolina State University, do not offer a major in biotechnology but do offer a minor. Yet universities change the majors they offer to adapt to the needs of industry. Thus, more schools will likely offer biotechnology majors in the near future.

Science fairs can offer opportunities to learn more about biotechnology and independent research. Here a middle school student shows off his award-winning project on frog cloning.

During college, students should continue to read about biotechnology and to attend lectures and workshops. Students should also complete one or more internships or work-study programs. An internship is an opportunity for a student to work in a laboratory with a more experienced researcher. Students can complete internships in a professor's lab on campus or off campus at a biotechnology company, hospital, or government laboratory.

Internships during the school year are usually part-time so that students can continue taking classes. Summer internships are often full-time positions. Internships can be paid or unpaid. Full-time internships usually include a salary. The pay won't be nearly as much as a researcher makes, but it is usually better than what would be earned in fast-food or campus jobs. Internships are sometimes available for high school students, but they are much more common for college students.

Graduate Degrees

Many positions are available to people with only bachelor's degrees. Positions with more responsibility and independence usually go to people with master's or doctoral degrees, however. Some master's programs focus on class work, while others combine classes and library and/or lab research. Writing a long research paper (known as a thesis) or taking a series of written and oral exams is generally required for graduation. Many universities now offer master's degrees in biotechnology. Some companies will allow employees to work part-time while pursuing a master's degree. In some cases, they even help pay for the additional education.

A few universities also offer programs that lead to a dual degree — a master of science in biotechnology and a master of business administration, or MBA degree. This combination of degrees is useful to students who are interested in working on the business side of biotechnology or opening their own biotechnology company.

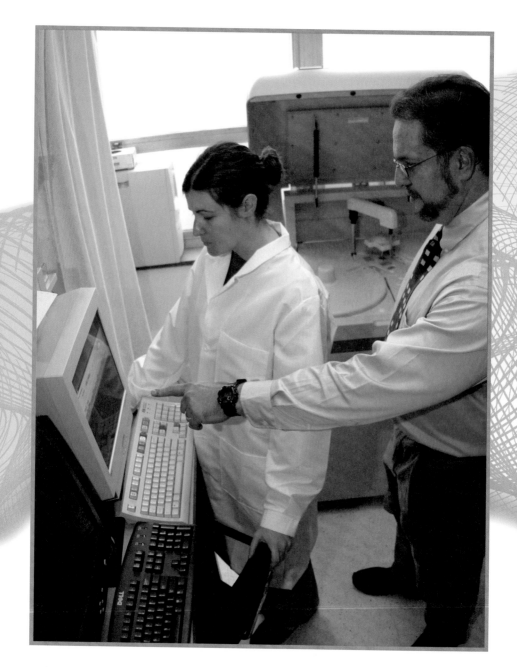

Universities offer many opportunities to perform research on critical problems in biotechnology. Here two researchers work on a clinical trial for a drug that is still in development.

Universities offering these dual-degree programs include Johns Hopkins University in Maryland, the University of Pennsylvania, the University of Florida, and the University of Calgary in Canada. Admission to MS/MBA programs often requires that you first gain two years of work experience after receiving a bachelor's degree.

A doctoral degree is also known as a Ph.D. It is the highest degree that someone can earn in a scientific field. Students do not have to earn a master's degree before completing a doctoral degree. In fact, some doctoral programs grant students a master's degree once they have completed certain requirements and while they continue working toward their Ph.D. Doctoral students take a few classes. Mostly they do independent research in a university laboratory. A professor serves as a research adviser. Before they graduate, doctoral students write a book-length research report about their work and conclusions. This is called a dissertation.

Doctoral students and master's students who conduct research write papers about their results that are sent to scientific journals. They also present their research to fellow academics at conferences. These graduate students may also help teach undergraduate courses and grade undergraduate papers and exams.

Depending on the field of study, it can take four to eight years—maybe longer—to earn a doctoral degree. Afterward, many people complete a post-doctoral fellowship, or post-doc. They spend one or two years in the lab of another university or a corporation. They generally work on a project different from the one upon which their dissertation was based. Completion of a post-doc is required to apply for many higher-level biotechnology jobs.

Students interested in biotechnology can earn a doctoral degree in any of the areas listed under undergraduate majors. Very few universities currently offer doctoral degrees in biotechnology. Two that do are Worcester Polytechnic Institute in Worcester, Massachusetts, and the University of Massachusetts. Some universities that do not offer graduate biotechnology degrees do offer specific training in biotechnology to graduate students who want it. This is called a designated emphasis or a concentration.

Earning a doctoral degree is a serious, long-range commitment, but it has many rewards. Doctoral degree holders earn more money than people with less education. They are also able to work more independently and be more creative. They often become the directors of research labs.

CHAPTER 4

Cutting Edge Careers
Cutting Edge Careers
Cutting Edge Careers

Bright Future, Lingering Controversies

Biotechnology is a rapidly expanding industry. Revenues from health-care biotechnology in the United States increased from $8 billion in 1992 to $39 billion in 2003, according to the Biotechnology Industry Organization. In 2005, 222 million acres in twenty-one countries were planted with biotechnology crops, according to the International Service for the Acquisition of Agri-biotech Applications.

The biotechnology industry is concentrated in particular regions, however. In 2002, the U.S. Department of Commerce Technology Administration and Bureau of Industry and Security conducted a survey of biotechnology companies. They found that 68 percent of the companies with fewer than 100 employees were located in just six states. These were

California, Massachusetts, Maryland, North Carolina, Pennsylvania, and New Jersey.

In the future, biotechnology companies may be spread more widely around the world. Countries such as China and India are strengthening their abilities in science and technology. People in some developing nations will work for lower salaries than those in the United States. Building offices, laboratories, and manufacturing plants is also cheaper in other nations. This could cause some American-based companies to decide to relocate. New start-up biotech companies may avoid the United States altogether. Currently, the United States is a leader in biotechnology research, but other countries are trying to catch up.

The 2002 survey of biotechnology companies by the U.S. Department of Commerce Technology Administration and Bureau of Industry and Security also asked about employees' jobs. Among technical employees of biotechnology companies:

— 6.2 percent were computer specialists focused on research and development

— 55.3 percent were scientists

— 8.3 percent were engineers

— 30.3 percent were technicians

Computer specialist was the fastest-growing technical occupation in the field of biotechnology. Few people have in-depth knowledge of both biology and computers. Those who do are in great demand.

Because the biotechnology industry is so focused on research and development, biotechnology could grow and change in ways that cannot yet be predicted. Much depends on what researchers discover is and is not possible, what the world's most pressing needs and

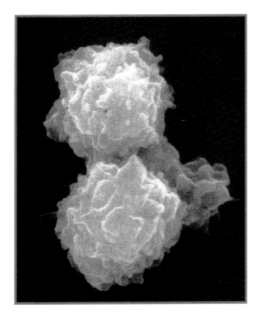

Stem cells such as these are useful because they can become any type of specialized cell in the body. Obtaining stem cells from embryos is controversial, however.

wants are, and what new products and technologies emerge from the laboratories. Because of this, in ten or twenty years, the in-demand jobs in biotechnology may be ones that do not exist today. In 2000, *Time* magazine predicted the ten hottest jobs of the twenty-first century. Four were related to biotechnology: tissue engineers, "frankenfood" monitors, gene programmers, and "pharmers."

Tissue engineers will use stem cells to create human organs and other tissues. Because these organs would contain the patient's DNA, researchers hope they would not be rejected by the body the way donor organs are. Rejection of transplanted organs can cause transplants to fail. There is also a chronic shortage of donor organs and long waiting lists of patients who need organs. So, any method for developing organs using the patient's own cells and DNA would be a great leap forward—one that could prolong and save thousands of lives.

"Frankenfood" is a word that critics of biotechnology sometimes use to refer to genetically modified organisms (GMOs). Frankenfood monitors will keep an eye on genetically modified plants and animals.

One of the major concerns regarding GMOs is that genetically modified crops will spread—via wind, birds, and foraging animals—beyond the boundaries of their farms and mix with wild populations and traditionally grown crops. Monitors will make sure that GMOs stay where they are supposed to be.

Gene programmers will use a computerized copy of a person's DNA to locate and identify possible problems that may lead to disease. Doctors will then be able to write personalized prescriptions of gene therapies and other drugs. These treatments may be able to prevent some cancers and other diseases that depend at least partly on genetics.

"Pharmers" will raise crops and livestock that have been genetically engineered to produce drugs and other medical treatments (the "ph" in pharmer comes from "pharmaceutical," another word for drug). These organisms contain foreign genes that cause them to make a lot of a certain protein or chemical, just like the bacteria used in industrial biotechnology. But instead of purifying the protein away from the bacteria, one can simply eat the plant or animal to gain the beneficial effects of the protein. Researchers are already growing tomatoes with vaccines in them and raising goats that produce milk that includes an anti-clotting drug.

Controversies in Agricultural Biotechnology

Biotechnology is a controversial field. Environmental groups, worried consumers, traditional farmers, and others have protested it. Some people refuse to buy bioengineered products. Politicians in many nations have made laws that restrict biotechnology research in certain areas. But biotechnology's reach continues to expand, despite such actions.

The safety of food produced using biotechnology is one source of controversy. Companies that create genetically modified organisms say that their products are substantially equivalent to—and often healthier than—foods that are not genetically engineered. Critics claim that these foods cannot be substantially equivalent because they have different DNA. No one knows what the long-term health effects of inserting genes from one organism into another may be. This is true for both the organism with the foreign gene, and for the people or animals that eat the genetically modified organism.

Food allergies are a particular concern. Some people become ill when they eat certain foods. They can break out in a rash or have trouble breathing. Some can even have a deadly reaction to certain foods, like peanuts. In many cases, researchers don't know what protein or proteins in the food cause the allergic reaction. If DNA from an allergy-causing food is put in another food that ordinarily causes no reaction in a person, the modified food may be consumed by that person—who remains unaware of the modification—and cause a dangerous reaction.

For example, scientists created genetically modified soybeans that contained a protein from a Brazil nut. They tested the soybeans on blood drawn from people who are allergic to Brazil nuts. The test showed that those people would have an allergic reaction to the soybeans as well. The soybeans were intended for chickens, not humans, to eat. The chickens digested the protein, so their meat did not cause allergic reactions in humans. But, to be safe, the company decided not to sell the soybeans containing the Brazil nut protein.

Containing the accidental spread of GMOs is also a controversial issue. People worry that genetically engineered organisms will get loose in the wild. Wind can easily transfer pollen from genetically modified plants to natural plants in a nearby field. Genetically modified animals can break out of their pens. Since the long-term health effects of genetic modification are still unknown, it would be a grave error if modified plants or animals began reproducing with "normal" plants and animals, passing on their genetic modifications to general populations.

Many products made without biotechnology promote this fact on their packaging.
This milk was made without hormones, antibiotics, or pesticides.

Finally, some people fear that insects and other pests will develop resistance to the pesticides genetically engineered into crops. While mutations in DNA can cause disease, sometimes they can lead to beneficial characteristics. Organisms can develop genetic mutations that make them immune to substances that are usually toxic. For example, some bollworms may develop a mutation that prevented the Bt in Bt cotton from hurting them. The bollworms with this characteristic would reproduce more than regular bollworms, since they would be more hardy and have access to a larger food supply than their unprotected cousins, which were still poisoned by Bt. Eventually, the pesticide in the cotton would not be effective anymore because the Bt-resistant bollworms would become dominant. Farmers currently plant fields of regular, non-modified plants near GMOs for the pests to feed on. This helps reduce the chances that they will develop resistance to the pesticides contained within the genetically modified crops.

Controversies in Health-Care Biotechnology

Biotechnology is a source of controversy in the health-care industry as well. The most intense debates surround cloning. Reproductive cloning is a difficult process. The nucleus of an egg cell is replaced with that from another cell of the body. This will create an exact genetic copy of that cell donor. The egg is coaxed to divide. The resulting embryo is then implanted in the womb, the embryo develops into a fetus, and the fetus is brought to term and delivered.

The success rate of reproductive cloning is less than 3 percent. Attempts to clone many animals have failed. Cloning a human being is likely to be even more difficult. In 2004, South Korean researchers claimed that they had cloned human embryos. A year later, the researchers were found to have faked their experiments. Research and experimentation related to human cloning is legal in many countries. Only time will tell whether it is possible.

Some governments have banned attempts to clone humans. Many people see cloning as unethical or worry that clones—who would be fully human, with an individual consciousness and personality—could be used for the "harvesting" of spare body parts.

Therapeutic cloning is also a controversial topic. It starts out the same way as reproductive cloning, by putting new DNA in an egg cell and causing it to develop into an embryo. But the embryo is not implanted into a womb. Instead, the embryo's stem cells are harvested to be implanted back into the original cell donor to cure a variety of diseases. Stem cells can be transformed into the cells of other organs, like the lung, liver, and kidney. So, they can be inserted into these organs to replace diseased cells. Stem cells that can change into other kinds of cells are rare in adult humans, however. Obtaining stem cells from cloned embryos or unused embryos in fertility clinics is far easier than obtaining them from adult bone marrow or fetal tissue.

Yet the process of extracting embryonic stem cells destroys the embryo. People who think that life begins at conception—when a sperm and egg join—consider harvesting stem cells from embryos to be murder. In August 2004, President George W. Bush decided that federal funds would be made available only for research on stem cell lines that were currently in existence. He would not support the destruction of any additional embryos to harvest stem cells. Companies, states, and nonprofit organizations still fund experiments on stem cells harvested from embryos after August 2004. All human embryonic stem cells have thus come from embryos provided by fertility clinics. Researchers have cloned embryonic stem cells in animals, but not yet in humans.

In addition, some people are concerned that biotechnology will someday allow parents to pick and choose their children's genes. Currently, doctors can test whether an unborn child will have certain

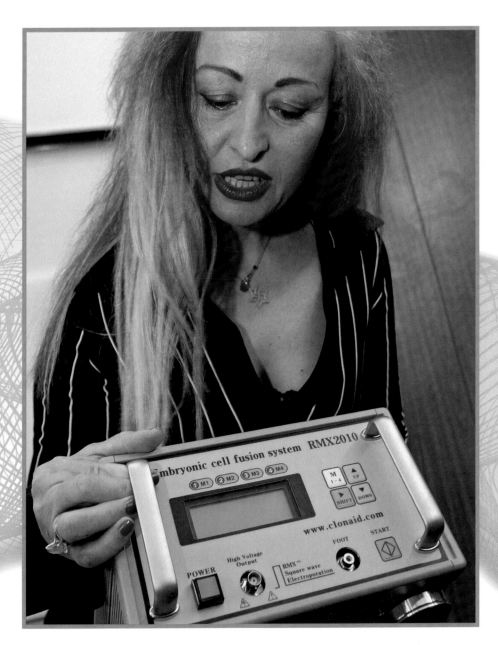

In 2003, a company called Clonaid claimed to have created five human clones using the embryonic cell fusion system seen here. Their claims were never proven, however, and are generally discounted as a hoax.

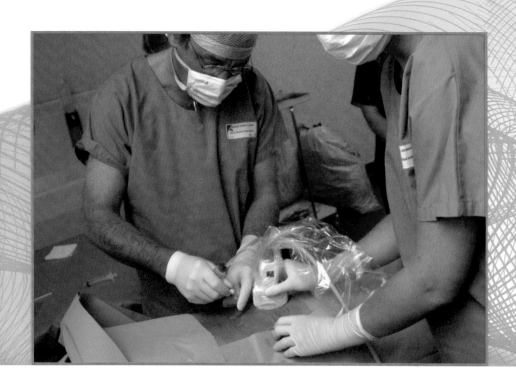

Doctors remove some of the fluid that surrounds an unborn child and test it for genetic diseases.

genetic diseases. Many people choose to abort children found to have genetic abnormalities. In the future, many people believe that researchers could create a child with a selected set of genes: high intelligence, athletic ability, beauty, or other traits thought to be positive and desirable. But creating a child "to order" would be expensive. This could lead to a divided society in which only wealthy people have genetically modified children. These children might be able to out-compete children born to less wealthy parents, further widening the gap between the "have's" and "have-not's."

Although various areas of biotechnology are controversial, the industry is still growing. Governments are likely to continue to pass laws regulating biotechnology. Some people will continue to refuse to eat genetically engineered food. But overall, applications of biotechnology will continue to expand. The genie cannot be put back into the bottle, and governments and society will have to find ways to harness biotechnology for the overall good of humanity.

As ethical and legal issues are debated and eventually resolved, and long-term health issues are studied and addressed, the often life-saving or life-extending processes and techniques that biotechnology can offer will come to the fore. The important, helpful, and amazing things biotechnology makes possible will become clearer, and its potential dangers or abuses will hopefully be curbed. Biotechnology is an exciting, hopeful, and dynamic field to enter—one in which you can have a long and stimulating career that has the potential to improve the quality of life on this planet for all living things.

GLOSSARY

associate's degree A degree awarded by a community or technical college after two years of study.

bachelor's degree A degree awarded after four years of study at a college or university.

bacteria Single-celled creatures that are used in biotechnology to produce useful products or carry out processes.

bioinformatics The use of computers to gain new information about DNA and protein.

biotechnology The use of living things to create processes, products, or services.

cell The basic unit of living things. Cells are tiny compartments that contain water, proteins, DNA, and other molecules.

clinical trial A test of a drug, vaccine, or other medical treatment on human beings.

DNA Short for deoxyribonucleic acid, DNA contains genes that carry the instructions to make proteins in the cell.

doctoral degree Also called a Ph.D., this advanced degree is awarded to holders of bachelor's degrees after four to eight years of additional study.

environmental biotechnology An area of biotechnology concerned with cleaning up pollution or solving other environmental issues.

enzyme A protein that makes chemical reactions proceed more quickly.

frankenfood A term sometimes used by critics of biotechnology to refer to genetically modified organisms.

gene A segment of DNA that contains instructions to make a protein.

gene therapy A method of treating genetic diseases. A healthy gene may replace a disease-causing gene, or supplement the unhealthy gene and reduce its effects.

genetically modified organism (GMO) An organism that has had its DNA changed in some way. Scientists may have removed or altered some of the organism's DNA, or may have added DNA from another organism.

genetic engineering The directed manipulation of genes.

herbicide A chemical that kills certain kinds of plants; primarily used on weeds.

industrial biotechnology The area of biotechnology that uses microorganisms to create useful products.

internship A paid or unpaid program in which a student works under supervision in a professional field (like a research laboratory) and gains practical experience.

master's degree An advanced degree awarded to holders of bachelor's degrees after one to two years of additional study.

microorganism A living creature that requires a microscope to be seen.

mutation A permanent change in an organism's DNA. Mutations can be harmful, beneficial, or have no effect.

organism A living thing.

patent A government document that gives the holder the exclusive right to manufacture and sell a product for a certain period of time.

pesticide A chemical that kills certain kinds of insects.

post-doctoral fellowship Also called a post-doc, this is one to two years of additional research and study undertaken after receiving a doctoral degree.

protein A molecule that performs work or a specialized task within the cell.

recombinant DNA technologies Technologies that allow researchers to break and rejoin DNA, and to make large quantities of it. This allows researchers to put new genes in an organism.

reproductive cloning The process of creating a living individual who has the same DNA as another individual.

research and development (R&D) The process in which researchers discover new knowledge and turn it into useful products, processes, and services.

therapeutic cloning The process of creating embryos from which researchers can remove stem cells for use in treating or curing certain diseases.

FOR MORE INFORMATION

American Chemical Society
1155 16th Street NW
Washington, DC 20036
(800) 227-5558
Web site: http://www.chemistry.org

BIOTECanada
130 Albert Street, Suite 420
Ottawa, ON K1P 5G4
Canada
(613) 230-5585
(416) 979-2652
Web site: http://www.biotech.ca

Biotechnology Institute
1840 Wilson Boulevard, Suite 202
Arlington, VA 22201
(703) 248-8687
Web site: http://www.biotechinstitute.org

Canadian Biotechnology Education Resource Centre (CBERC)
MaRS Centre, Heritage Building
101 College Street, Suite 120-E
Toronto, ON M5G 1L7
Canada

(416) 673-8471
Web site: http://www.cberc.ca

Council for Biotechnology Information
1225 I Street NW, Suite 400
Washington, DC 20005
(202) 962-9200
Web site: http://www.whybiotech.com

Institute on Biotechnology and the Human Future
565 W. Adams Street
Chicago, IL 60661
(312) 906-5337
Web site: http://www.thehumanfuture.org

National Center for Biotechnology Information
National Library of Medicine
Building 38A
8600 Rockville Pike
Bethesda, MD 20894
(301) 496-2475
Web site: http://www.ncbi.nih.gov

Society for Industrial Microbiology
3929 Old Lee Highway, Suite 92A
Fairfax, VA 22030-2421
(703) 691-3357
Web site: http://www.simhq.org

Web Sites

Due to the changing nature of Internet links, Rosen Publishing has developed an online list of Web sites related to the subject of this book. This site is updated regularly. Please use this link to access the list:

http://www.rosenlinks.com/cec/biot

FOR FURTHER READING

Cassedy, Patrice. *Biotechnology*. San Diego, CA: Lucent Books, 2003.

Creative Media Applications. *A Student's Guide to Biotechnology*. Westport, CT: Greenwood Press, 2002.

Fridell, Ron. *Genetic Engineering*. Minneapolis, MN: Lerner Publishing Group, 2006.

Jefferis, David. *Biotech: Frontiers of Medicine*. New York, NY: Crabtree, 2002.

Morgan, Sally. *Superfoods: Genetic Modification of Foods*. Chicago, IL: Heinemann Library, 2002.

Nardo, Don. *Cloning*. San Diego, CA: Lucent Books, 2002.

Parker, Steve. *Genetic Engineering*. Chicago, IL: Raintree, 2005.

Richardson, Hazel. *How to Clone a Sheep*. New York, NY: Franklin Watts, 2001.

BIBLIOGRAPHY

"Access Excellence." National Health Museum. 2005. Retrieved April 13, 2006 (http://www.accessexcellence.org).

Bains, William. *Biotechnology from A to Z*. 3rd ed. New York, NY: Oxford University Press, 2004.

BioSpace. "BioSpaceJobs." Biospace.com. 2006. Retrieved April 13, 2006 (http://www.biospace.com/jobs).

Bush, George W. "President Discusses Stem Cell Research." WhiteHouse.gov. 2001. Retrieved April 17, 2006 (http://www.whitehouse.gov/news/releases/2001/08/20010809-2.html).

Business Insights. "Healthcare Reports: The Top 10 Biotechnology Companies." GlobalBusinessInsights.com. 2005. Retrieved April 14, 2006 (http://www.globalbusinessinsights.com/report.asp?id=rbhc0140).

"Career Voyages." U.S. Department of Labor and U.S. Department of Education. 2006. Retrieved April 12, 2006 (http://www.careervoyages.gov).

"Cloning scientist: Forgive me." CNN.com. 2006. Retrieved April 16, 2006 (http://www.cnn.com/2006/HEALTH/01/11/skorea.stemcell/index.html).

"Council for Biotechnology Information." Council for Biotechnology Information. 2004. Retrieved April 12, 2006 (http://www.whybiotech.com).

Counsell, Damian. "Bioinformatics Frequently Asked Questions." Bioinformatics.org. 2004. Retrieved April 15, 2006 (http://bioinformatics.org/faq).

Education Committee. "Careers in Industrial Microbiology and
Biotechnology." Society for Industrial Microbiology. 1997.
Retrieved April 11, 2006 (http://www.simhq.org/html/
careersindustrial.html).

"Golden Rice." Golden Rice Humanitarian Board. 2006. Retrieved
April 14, 2006 (http://www.goldenrice.org).

"ISAAA Briefs No. 34-2005: Executive Summary." International
Service for the Acquisition of Agri-Biotech Applications. 2005.
Retrieved April 12, 2006 (http://www.isaaa.org/kc/bin/briefs34/
es/index.htm).

"LifeWorks." National Institutes of Health Office of Science Education.
2006. Retrieved April 12, 2006 (http://science.education.nih.gov/
LifeWorks).

National Research Council Committee on Defining Science-Based
Concerns Associated with Products of Animal Biotechnology.
Animal Biotechnology: Science-Based Concerns. Washington, DC:
National Academies Press, 2002.

"Northwest Biotechnology/Biomedical Education and Careers
Consortium." Northwest Biotechnology/Biomedical Education
and Careers Consortium. 2002. Accessed April 3, 2006 (http://
success.shoreline.edu/NWBBEC).

Office of Biological and Environmental Research, Human Genome
Program. "Cloning Fact Sheet." U.S. Department of Energy Office
of Science. 2006. Retrieved April 11, 2006 (http://www.ornl.gov/
sci/techresources/Human_Genome/elsi/cloning.shtml).

"Posilac: Bovine Somatotropin by Monsanto." Monsanto. 2005.
Retrieved April 14, 2006 (http://www.monsantodairy.com).

"Preparing for a Biotech Career." North Carolina Biotechnology
Center. Retrieved April 3, 2006 (http://www.ncbiotech.org/
careers/jobresc/prepare.cfm).

"Resource Library." Amgen. 2005. Retrieved April 15, 2006 (http://
www.amgen.com/science/resource_library.html).

Rowe, Julie. "What Will Be the 10 Hottest Jobs?" *Time*, May 22, 2000.

"The Scientist Careers." *The Scientist*. 2006. Retrieved April 12, 2006 (http://careers.the-scientist.com).

"Talking Glossary of Genetic Terms." National Institutes of Health National Human Genome Research Institute. Retrieved April 14, 2006 (http://www.genome.gov/10002096).

U.S. Department of Commerce Technology Administration and Bureau of Industry and Security. *A Survey of the Use of Biotechnology in U.S. Industry*. Washington, DC: GPO, 2003.

Weintraub, Arlene. "Gene Therapy Is Respectable Again." *BusinessWeek*, December 5, 2005, p. 76.

INDEX

About the Author

Linley Erin Hall is a science writer and editor in San Francisco, California, one of the major biotechnology centers in the United States. She has a B.S. degree in chemistry, with an emphasis on biochemistry from Harvey Mudd College and a certificate in science communication from the University of California–Santa Cruz. She performed research in a biochemistry lab as an undergraduate and has written about many biology-related topics. This is Hall's third book for Rosen Publishing.

Photo Credits

Cover top © Bertrand Collet/www.istockphoto.com; cover bottom © Getty Images; pp. 4–5 © Bruce Rolff/Shutterstock; p. 6 National Human Genome Research Institute; p. 7 © David Greedy/Getty Images; p. 11 © Indranil Mukherjee/AFP/Getty Images; p. 14 © Scott Olson/Getty Images; p. 16 © Michael Smith/Getty Images; p. 20 Keith Weller/USDA; p. 23 © Gary Williams/Getty Images; p. 27 © Desirey Minkoh/AFP/Getty Images; p. 29 © T. Bannor/Custom Medical Stock Photo, Inc.; p. 31 © Peter Chen/www.istockphoto.com; p. 33 © Laurence Gough/Shutterstock; p. 36 © Gannett Rochester, Karen Schiely/AP/Wide World Photos; p. 38 © Jordan Silverman/Getty Images; p. 43 © JI Carson/Custom Medical Stock Photo, Inc.; p. 46 © Ben Margot/AP/Wide World Photos; p. 49 © David Silverman/Getty Images; p. 50 © AJPhoto/Photo Researchers, Inc.

Series Designer: Evelyn Horovicz; Photo Researcher: Hillary Arnold